The Night Light

by Winston White
illustrated by Alan Flinn

 HOUGHTON MIFFLIN

BOSTON

Jerry climbed into bed. His mother kissed him and turned out the light. Then she plugged in the night light. It happened the same way every night.

Jerry wished he didn't need the night light.
But he was afraid of the dark. Without the night
light, he thought about scary things under the
bed. He thought about scary things in the closet.
When Jerry saw the night light, he thought about
sleeping.

One day at school, Kevin handed a note to Jerry. "My birthday is tomorrow," said Kevin. "I'm having a sleepover. I hope you can come, Jerry."

Jerry mumbled, "I'll have to check with my mom." He already knew he wouldn't go to the sleepover. How could he take his night light with him? All the other boys would laugh at him.

So Jerry didn't go to Kevin's sleepover.

One day at a scout meeting, Mr. Price, the scoutmaster, talked about an overnight camping trip. All the scouts were excited about the trip—all except Jerry.

Mr. Price gave each boy a sheet of paper. "Please have your parents read this and sign it. Then you can go camping," said Mr. Price.

Jerry folded the paper and put it in his pocket. How could he camp out at night in the dark? Even if he wanted to take along his night light, there was no place to plug it in.

He would have to skip the camping trip too.

That night, Jerry's father said, "It looks like we're in for some bad weather. I'll get some candles ready."

Soon, a big storm rumbled in. Lightning flashed, and thunder cracked. The lights in the house dimmed once, twice, and then went out!

Jerry didn't like the dark one bit. He could hardly wait until his father lit the candles.

Then he thought of his dark bedroom. There would be no night light tonight.

At eight o'clock, there was a knock on the door. "It's Granddad," called a voice. Granddad lived in the apartment upstairs.

"I've come to say good night to Jerry," said Granddad with a wink. He knew how Jerry felt about the dark.

Together, they went to Jerry's bedroom. "Jerry, I know you don't like the dark," said Granddad. "I didn't like it either when I was a child. But my mother helped me."

"How?" asked Jerry.

Granddad explained. "One night, my mother sat by my bed. It was very dark. She opened the curtains at the window. There was the moon, shining its bright light into my room. My mother told me to look for the moon whenever I was afraid of the dark."

"But you can't always see the moon, Granddad. Especially on a stormy night like tonight," Jerry said.

"The moon is never gone, Jerry. It's always up there in the sky, waiting to shine its light. Sometimes you just have to wait," answered Granddad.

As he spoke, Jerry and Granddad looked out
the window. The moon came out from behind
the clouds. Its bright light shone into Jerry's
room.

"There is your night light, Jerry," Granddad said.

"Thanks, Granddad," whispered Jerry, hugging his grandfather.

The next morning, Jerry asked his mother to sign the paper for the scouts' camping trip.

Jerry went camping that weekend. And at night, he looked for his new night light in the sky!